CODE NAME: AXEL

By
MARK W. LESLIE

Prelude
Someone's Big City USA

Darkness, at what appears to be an old house in the dead of night. Moving down a hallway towards a door at the end, a loud yell and a slash echo from the other side, then a name is screamed **"Cj!!"** the door opens and a young girl's voice yells out **"Dj!!"** a flash of light then darkness.

Her eyes opens, and her heart rate and pressure are up, but she ignores it. From her earpiece, a voice speaks "Axel, Axel, hey Axel. Cj! Cj! baby girl! you're there?" Then she gently presses the piece and answers, "I'm here F." F says the mission's a bust. Agent Capricorn needs aid. Your orders are to move in and assist. Axel says, "Orders received, moving to assist." She grabs her gear and prepares to recline down the large hotel she's on. As she leaps off the rooftop, another voice sounds off from her earpiece,

"Agent Axel, this is Colonel Piedmont. You have new orders. I repeat, you have new orders. Clear, sweep, and clean. I say again clear, sweep and clean."

"F" speaks up "But Colonel, what about agent Capricorn?"

Piedmont answers "Stand down F, Capricorn has been compromised Axel, you have your orders."

Axel replies "Roger that Colonel." she swings toward a window, and clashes through "CLASH!!" as she lands inside a room, she grabs both of her pistols and fires at five goons surrounding agent Capricorn, who's been slapped around a bit "BANG, BANG, BANG" two goons fall as the others duck and covers. CLICK, CLICK, CLICK, she out of rounds, she quickly unhooks from her gear as one of the goons rushes at her, she reaches for her katana and says to it,

"Sunflower you are needed." she ducks under the goon's punch then slashes a large gash across his back, he falls to the floor as a second goon charge at her with a knife, she blocks it and rams Sunflower through his chest. The third goon pulls out two long blades he swings them all around his chest, and stares at her.

Axel says "Sunflower, is he challenging us?" The goon gives her the swordsman salute as he raises one of the blades to his head. Axel returns the salute and says, "A duel then." they both smile, then charge each other. "TING! TING! CLINK! the swords meet, then they back away from each other, Axel looks at Sunflower and says, "You slut. You like both of them." the goon looks puzzled hearing her speak to her sword. He charges again, and the blades clash "KA-CLING!" DING!" the goon slices upwards, cutting the side of her face "Ouch!" she yells, he powers kicks her in the chest, which knocks her hard into the dresser behind her, shattering it. As she lays on the floor, she thinks to herself *"That hurts everywhere."*

The goon moves in on her for the kill. She thinks *"I've only got seconds."* as she pulls out a small digger saying to it, "Daisy, you are needed." The goon starts to swing down with his sword over her, but she punches Daisy through his foot, causing him to yell, and fall back enough for her to move to better ground. She grabs Sunflower saying, "Let's finish this." She rams Sunflower through the goon's chest, then runs it upwards toward his throat. As he falls to the floor, the first goon with the slashed back runs for the door, she grabs her digger saying, "Daisy, get him." she throws it so hard that the blade punches through the back of his head to the front. His body falls to the floor.

Agent Capricorn jumps from the bed runs over to Axel and hugs her as she cries "Axel!" "Axel, you saved me!" "Thank you, thank you!" "They were going to kill me!" Axel doesn't say a word as Capricorn continues "I, I can't." "I can't do this anymore." I just can't, I want out." Axel says, "I know." Capricorn pauses and pulls back from her as she notices the sound of Axel's voice, then she steps back as she sees Axel's expression she asks, "Cj what's w..." Capricorn's words are interrupted as Axel swings Sunflower taking a chunk out of her throat causing her to choke on her own blood. Unable to speak, or breathe, she grabs her throat trying to stop the bleeding.

She falls to her knees looking up, and her eyes ask the question her mouth can't. Axel answers,

"Because you fail sister." "The goons here weren't trying to kill you." "You were feeding them information." "You were selling out the Agency, Wasn't you?"

Tears flow from Capricorn's eyes as her body starts to fall to the floor, Axel catches her and eases her down. Tears flow from Axel as she says "I'm so sorry sister, but you broke the code, and I have my orders." She takes Daisy and slowly drives it into Capricorn's chest as she says "Shhhh sister, embrace the darkness then go to the light." "I will join you soon." "I love you." Capricorn's eyes close as her life force fades away. Axel cries.

Chapter I

Reality Check

A few minutes passed as she continues crying and holding Capricorn's body. Finally, she gets a call from F. "Axel? Axel?! Cj!" he yells.

Then the call from the Colonel rings in "Agent Axel, report! I repeat report. Now!" Axel gently presses her earpiece and answers "The area is cleared and swept sir."

F answers "I'm sorry Cj. You and Capricorn were so close." she replies "Yeah, yeah we were."

Colonel Piedmont interrupts "Ah enough of the mushy shit! Continue to phase two, then get the hell out of there!" she answers "Roger,".

Minutes later after she has placed all the bodies in the bathtub, she starts spraying them with a chemical compound that starts to dissolve them down to a melted and unrecognized state. Now she sprays a second compound which dissolves away all the many fingerprints that would be found in the room. As she cleans the blood from her blades the front door opens, three men in full white hazmat suits walks in, and the lead steps up to her saying,

"We'll take it from here agent."

She nods her head as she heads back to the busted window, she looks back d seeing more men entering the room, two of them are carrying a replacement window. She grips and reconnects her gear, gently presses the earpiece, and says "F., I need you." as she jumps out pulling upwards towards the rooftop F answers "I'm always here for you baby girl."

Demons, many of us seem to have them, and while so many of us are unaware, some of us know and understand that we can find ourselves daily in a continuous battle with our very own demon, or demons.
For Axel, the battle with hers rages onward hourly and almost nonstop, only getting breaks when she's on missions

killing, as she creates even more demons for her to battle.
For even now she can hear the yelling, the screaming, the sounds of **"Cj!"** **"Nooooo!"** she sees the flash of light then darkness.
She jumps as her eyes open. She hears F speak "Cj? Cj? You alright?" she shakes her head and says "I'm fine. Why you ask?" he answers,

"Well you look dazed and confused, plus you jumped as you keep saying no, no, no. So, I guess you were having that nightmare again."

She stares at him saying, "I'm fine, continue your work." he huffs saying "Okay then. Lay back in the chair and turn your head so I can see it better." "Yeah. That's a nasty cut babe. from your ear down the jaw to your chin. He huffs again saying "That may leave a very nasty scare. Well let's see what we can do to fix you up." he grabs a small device and starts to activate it as Axel opens her eyes asking,

"What is that?" F responds "Oh this is one of my new toys. It emits a blue light." she cuts him off saying "A blue light? What is its function? He answers, "Well babe, the blue light freezes the skin so that area is completely numb, so you won't feel any pain as I stitch you up." She asks, "Did you make it?" He replies, "Well I drew it up, but Axel Grease Monkey built it." She responds, "Hmmm, How is his name is also Axel?"

He answers, "Well while Axel is your code name, it's his real name. Since he does all the mechanical works for the Agency we gave him the name Grease Monkey. I'm surprised you haven't met him yet, as long as you been with us." Almost smiling she says, "I would really like to meet the Monkey Grease Axel."

He replies, "Uh yea, okay be still so I can get started. At first, it's gonna feel real cold in the area it touches, then you won't feel a thing for about an hour. No Pain." as she starts to feel the icy cold on her face she utters "I think I like the pain." he replies "I know that's what I'm afraid of. Now be quiet and still. I have to do some of my best work to fix this mess of a cut you got this time."

Sometime later F speaks "There, all done. You know babe you get to be more careful. If anything were to happen to you...well, you know how I feel about you… she cuts him off "F stop it. You know we can never be together."

She gets up and turns away from him saying "We can't ever have what we truly want." He huffs saying "Okay I'll stop. By the way, I don't know how well that cut is going to heal. It may leave you with a nasty scare."

She replies, "That's fine, it's just another medal for my body to display. Where did they take Capricorn's remains."

He answers, "Where they take all our fallen agents' remains…To **The Place**."

He continues "You know there's not much left of her. You should go home and get some rest." she responds, "I will rest, after I pay my respects to my friend." she walks out of the room, not once did she look back at him. F huffs as he whispers to himself,

"Yeah babe. love you too."

About five minutes later, Piedmont enters saying, "There you are F. Where's agent Axel?"

F answers "I sent her home, she needs to get some rest." the colonel asks,

"Well, what's her status? Is she ready for another mission?" F answers, "Well she has some cuts and bruises. Plus, she's not happy about being ordered to kill her friend…" Piedmont cuts him off saying,

"Nuts to all that man! Is she ready for another mission? We get a live one this time!"

F yells, "You're not hearing me colonel? She's not ready yet for another of your one-offs, seek and kill everyone murder runs, you call missions! It's too soon!"

The colonel in rage says, "Look F, you need to get your foolish heart out of her panties, and start to understand that the woman that keeps your pee-wee hard, is nothing more than a well-trained, killing machine! One day you're gonna find out just how cold-hearted she truly is when you're on the other side of her blade fading into darkness after she just sliced the life out of you."

F responds, "How dare you speak to me that way!" The colonel says "I have my orders. Now you have yours. Get your head out of her ass, and have her here at 0800 tomorrow, ready to go to work."

As the colonel starts to leave he turns back at F and saying, "0800 F, be on time, and that's an order." he leaves as F finds himself full of anger he lashes out by slapping some items off his desk.

After a moment or two to calm down he sees that he has knocked over a picture of him and Cj,

"Oh no!" he thinks to himself then he takes a good look at it as he begins to remember the time they had just a few years ago. He thinks *"Dam Cj I still remember that day on the beach. When you weren't afraid to share your feelings with me. You weren't so guarded, so distant, so lost. Dam baby I miss you so much."*

He picks up the picture and places it back on the desk as he leaves the room.

Sometime later at "The Place"

It's a simple place where the Agency's fallen agents are laid to rest...well what's left of them anyway.

Axel is standing by the spot where the remains of her friend Agent Capricorn have been placed, along with the goons she killed earlier. Tears began to fall from her eyes. She speaks,

"I'm so sorry sister. I didn't want this, but I had no choice. You just can't leave the agency. The things they would have done to you if I hadn't killed you. They would have made you a mindless slave, or worse, a weapon, a killer, a murderer…Like me, you would never know peace. I couldn't let you fall like that...Like I have."

She closes her eyes the salt from her tears starts to burn the new scar on her face. she thinks to herself "Dam Capri I still remember when we first met. Our training together, our first mission, our many talks, and dreams we shared, and now...now your,,,?

She hears a sound then an eerie voice **"Cj."** she thinks as she opens her eyes *"That voice?, Sounds like Capri."* the voice speaks again but louder **"Cj."** she thinks *"Now I know where it's coming from."* she grabs Sunflower as she turns to face the voice placing it inches away from the face of the voice behind her

"Uh we really should stop meeting like this babe." the voice says Axel relax as she put her sword away saying "Oh F it's you." she continues "You should be more careful, I could have killed you...I done enough killing for one night."

F responds, "I told you to go home and get some rest." she drops her head and says, "I can't." he gently places his hand under her chin, he raises her head so their eyes connect,

"Cj, Capri is gone now. There's nothing you...we can do for her now. The colonel has a mission for you, at 0800." she lends toward him speaking in his ear, "I need you tonight." she walks away as he smiles,

"I'm always here for you babe!" he says as he heads to catch up with her.

Years ago, inside a very large cave, somewhere in South Korea.

In the large opening, and well-lit area twelve young children. They appear to range between the ages of twelve to fifteen. They're kneeling with their heads bowed and hands placed on their knees. Each one has a cloth in front of them with both a sword and dagger lying on it.

Just above them are large balconies filled with what appear to be high-ranking military men from many countries. They're looking down on the children with high anticipation. Then darkness dreams her eyes opens. She jumps as she awakes from her dream, she looks to her right, she sees F sitting in the chair next to her bed,

"Another bad dream?" he asked, she replies as she turns over away from him "I don't want to talk about it." He responds "Babe sooner or later you must talk about it. That's the only way you'll defeat the demons that haunts your dreams every night. They won't stop until you do."

She answers,"Right now, I want you to stop F." He replies "As you wish, you know I would do anything for you babe. Kiss you, watch over you as you sleep. Hell, I'll fall on your sword if you ask me to. Whatever it takes to make you happy."

She says, "Then you won't have to do much, because nothing can make me happy. I can never be happy., Happiness is not for me." She closes her eyes as a tear rolls down her cheek.

F says, "I'm sorry Cj, I'll let you get back to sleep." He thinks to himself *"What can I do to help the woman I love? Dam I feel so helpless."*

0:800 Agency Headquarters, Location Room number 8 the Briefing Room

Axel and F are sitting waiting for the colonel. Neither of them has spoken to each other since last night, F thinks to himself,

"Well I guess I have to be the one to break the Ice." he asks, "Hey babe did you sleep better after your halftime last night?"

She answers "As best as I could. How long did you stay up?"

He replies saying,"I don't remember when I blanked out, but I didn't sleep long, you know me."

She cuts him off saying, "Well uh..." "Don't...Don't. I do not want to talk about it."

"Alright, alright." he reacts just as the door opens and in walks Colonel Piedmont and two others. Piedmont speaks,

"Alex, F this is Agent Bart Campbell, and his daughter Agent Bella." "They're some of the Agency's best overseas operatives.

Bart shakes hands with F as he speaks "Agent F. I heard so much about you." Then he focused his eyes on "Agent Axel. America's top assassin, it is a pleasure to finally meet you."

Cj nods her head at both agents as a slight pause covers the room F breaks the silence "Campbell and Campbell. I heard so much about you two." I've studied some of your cases. Bart answers,

"Good then you should be acquainted with the international assassin the Empress." Bella says, "We've been tracking her work for some time now."

Bewildered F looks over to the colonel as he sees him looking back with a smirk on his face. F asks, "Wait isn't the Empress an international target? We only deal with stateside targets."

Piedmont sits back in his chair rubbing his hands saying, "You're in the big leagues now boy."

Bart interrupts "As the colonel eloquently put it. We've tracked her to the States, she's here for her new target she's been hired to take out."

Bella adds, "Yes and since she's now playing in our yard, we have the home-field advantage."

Bart continues "And we want to make this a welcoming that she'll never forget."

The Colonel smiles as F speaks "Wow a chance to take down the Empress. I had a feeling that this would come someday, that's why I've keeping tabs on her for some time myself."

He, looks at Axel asking, "What do you think babe? You're up to it?"

She looks at him, she looks around the room answering "Yes, let's get to it. Who is her target?"

Bart answers, "Oh, well I'm the target." Bella drops her head as those words pierce through her heart like a missile. Bart continues, "Oh, yeah I've done some much damage, and distractions to our enemies, that someone finally decided to cash in my chips." "The good part is that the Empress is a game piece we've been waiting to remove off the board for some time now."

Bella adds, "That's why we came to you two because the word is you're the best."

F replies, "Yes we are the best. Cj is the best." "Where's the showdown going down?

Bart answers "The Oasis Metropolis Mall." "And since I'm the target I guess, I'm the bate as well. And as bate, she will reveal herself once I'm out in the open then you guys can take it from there…right?

Colonel Piedmont answers "Of course Agent Campbell you have nothing to fear.

Campbell responds, "Yeah uh what you said"

Axel asks, "When do we mobilize?

Campbell answers, "As soon as you're ready my dear."

Everyone begins to leave the room except Axel and F who continues to study the flies. Axel notices that Bella is still standing at the door she thinks to herself *I think Agent Campbell wants to speak to me*" She looks at F saying "I need some time alone F.

He replies, "Oh, uh alright. I'll see you in a little bit babe. He leaves as Bella approaches Axel, she speaks,

"Agent Axel I heard about Agent Capricorn."

Axel just stares at her in silence. Bella continues "It must have been hard for you to kill your friend. You must have a high sense of duty."

Axel finally answers, "What do you want of me, Agent Campbell?"

Bella sighs and answers, "Well, yeah. The Empress is very, very good at what she does, and my father is not the agent he once was. I'm asking, I'm begging you to keep my father safe from that witch's blade."

Axel stands looking into Bella's eyes saying, "I will do all I can to protect your father." As Axel leaves the room Bella thinks to herself *"Yeah, I pray you do."*

Moments later Bella catches up with her father he asks, "So what you think?" she answers, "There's something very tragic about her. Something so dark, so, well I can't seem to figure it out, but I'm not too sure about her." As he begins to ponder her word she continues "Father are you sure you want to go on with this? There must be another way."

He answers, "This is the only play we have Sugar Plum. And I intend to meet the Empress head-on no matter the risk."

The Oasis Metropolis Mall
owned by O Enterprises

It's a very large shopping complex, full of stores, restaurants, hotels, movie theaters, arcades, and other such entertainments. But unknown to the public, it's also a safe haven for many of our nation's government agents. Although on any giving day, there may be a ton of agents secretly enjoying some much-needed R and R. Today there are way more agents here than usual, and they are not here to shop or check out the latest blockbuster at the movies, no they're here for business.

Other than the extra gun power the place is full of life, colors, and sounds, yes capitalism is in full effect here.

But in one of the many hidden rooms in total darkness, Axel awaits her blind date with the Empress. As she waits for orders to move, she battles with her demons,

"Please, please, leave me you cursed-ed nightmares. Go away, please go away."

F calls her on the earpiece "Cj. Cj. You okay?" she answers, "I'm here F, I'm fine."

He responds, "Good cause I think the Empress has just entered the building." "The colonel wants you ready, babe."

She answers I'm moving into position. And don't call me that."

In the middle of this amazing building sitting out in the open are the Campbells waiting for the rat to trip the trap.

Bella speaks "Daddy? Daddy. Daddy! He answers, "What Sugar Plum." she replies, "I don't like you being out in the open like this. Couldn't you think of a better plan than this?" He answers "I wanted to keep it simple this time, and besides I'm not afraid of her, or anyone else out to get me. Relax Sugar Plum.

Everything will work out fine, you'll see." She insists "But daddy out in the open like this. Not only are you putting yourself in danger, but you're also risking the lives of so many others."

He replies, "Sugar Plum, you know that risk is part of the game. If the risk to high, you can't play this game. Every agent learns that on day one."

He places his hand on her cheek and says, "Sugar Plum all will be well, you'll see. Trust me." he smiles saying "Now look sharp, I believe that the lion is here to claim her prize."

Bella smiles saying, "Yes sir" but she thinks *"Dam. Daddy I hope you're right because I just can't shake the thought that this is the last time we talk."*

She's been walking through the massive building for some time now. Her head is covered with a hood, her face painted with the marking of her clan armed with a sword, daggers, and pistols all hidden underneath her ropes and cape she is ready for whatever comes her way.

As she closes in on her target most of the people who notice her start to head back to their hotel rooms or their cars in the nearby parking lot. Then there's the others who just standing there watching not believing that a raw deal is about to go down.

She thinks to herself,

"Rats. Look at all the rats, hiding among the people. They think I don't know which ones are the rats, and which are the people. They don't know that I can see them as they start, slowly closing in on me. They must think me the fool. They will all learn from my teaching. A lesson that none of them will ever forget. There they are the Campbells. The cheese to this sorry ass trap."

She walks towards them as two undercover agents move toward her reaching for their pistols she thinks,

"So these are the first rats to fall by my blade this day." she grabs her sword and quickly slashes the two as their bodies fall to the floor innocent bystanders begin running and screaming as some more agents fight through the crowds toward the Empress. She slashes down the crest of one agent and rams a dagger through the forehead of another as a 3rd fires his pistol she dodges and throws a dagger into his neck dropping him.

Jokingly Bart stands up saying "See Sugar Plum, just as I thought." Bella yells "Daddy stop playing and start shooting."

Both fires at the Empress, she rolls and dives for cover dropping two more agents with her pistol. Two agents rush to her hidden area as she has not moved since she reached that spot.

Bart yells "Get out of the way you fools are blocking our line of fire."

Just as he spoke Empress swings her sword through the throat of the first agent and quickly turns and fire into the belly of the other. She runs as other agents take aim at her.

Bart yells out, "I'm chasing her down Sugar Plum, and you head her off at the pass!" he winks at her as he runs after Empress.

Bella answers, "This isn't one of your old western movies, Daddy! Daddy!"

But he's way passed the range of hearing her clearly.

He thinks, "Just do as *"I say Sugar Plum. All will work out fine."*

As the Empress runs, she fires at her enemies. Agents fall one by one, two by two they fall like raindrops on a stormy day they fall. She rushes up the escalator to the second floor.

Bart follows her up but not as impressive. Running up a second escalator Bella yells through her earpiece,

"Piedmont, where's the hell are your people?! That bitch is gonna kill my father!! Do something now!!!"

Bart adds, "Yeah Colonel I can't keep her pinned down for long, this bitch ain't playing she just dropped three more agents. So, let's make with some swordplay of our own shell we?"

Bella yells out, "I'm coming Daddy!"

Piedmont yells, "F! Get your asses in the game Now!" F acknowledge, "Rodger that Colonel." he calls "Cj! Cj! Where are you girl?!"

Standing on the fourth floor on the other side of the mall Axel can see all that's taken place she answers F, "I'm moving in."

Using a mini glider, she jumps from the edge of the fourth gliding toward the second floor. She can see Bart with double pistols shooting at the Empress who's hiding behind cover, but she can tell that the Empress is about to strike.

Empress throws a dagger at Bart, he tries to block it using one of his pistols, giving her time to move in close, she slashes another agent and swings her blade toward Bart's chest, he's able to block it with his other pistol, she leg sweeps him off his feet, while falling he drops both pistols once he lands he reaches for one of them, but she rams a dagger through his hand causing him to yell out in pain.

He looks up at her and just as she is about to strike with her sword Axel dives into Empress and the ladies roll about ten to fifteen feet away from Bart as he struggles to pull the dagger out of his hand the ladies face off.

Empress still with her head covered by her hood thinks to herself *"Finally."*

Axel speaks, "Sunflower, I need you." as she draws her sword.

Empress addresses Axel "So you are still using that slut of a blade Sunflower, I guess you are still using Daisy as well eh sister?"

Every word she spoke brought a chill down Axel's back as she started to realize who she was facing.

"It can not be."

"Yes, sister it is I. You thought me to be dead did you Cj?"

Hearing everything over the earpiece chills runs down F's back as he too realizes that something's wrong. He thinks *"What the hell!"* he jumps up from his station and runs out of the room "I got to get out there."

Axel speaks in shock, "Aj? You are alive?"

 "Yes Cj, I am here to change your life, dear sister." Axel raises her sword, laughing Empress says, "Hahaha You know you could never beat me in a fair fight."

Axel yells as she swings Sunflower at Empress who blocks it with her sword

"Cj I like you to meet my new blade "Dragon Bane.""

The two ladies clash their swords into each other over, and over again until Empress forces Axel to over swing allowing Empress to elbow Axel in the back of her head, she stumbles as Empress rakes Dragon Bane across her lower back.

In pain Axel rises her body Empress kicks her in the back causing Axel to fall face first to the floor dropping sunflower as well.

Empress quickly jumps back towards Bart as he just finally removed the dagger from his hand as he stands up bleeding out of his left hand pointing his one pistol with the other hand he says, "Bitch you should be out of daggers by now."

Empress answers, "You would think so." she throws two daggers from her sleeves one hitting Bart in his neck, and the other in his chest causing him to stubble back into the rails alone the edge, he tries to fire his pistol, but she runs Dragon Bane though his wrist cutting his hand clean off Bart yells in pain as Bella final arrives she sees Axel on the floor bleeding and her father press against the rail she runs toward him Yelling,

"Daddy! Daddy!"

He looks into the Empress's eyes as she stares at him, he asks, "Who...who paid...you?"

She answers, "The Big Man sends his regards." she smiles.

Bart also smiling replies, "Big...Man... that bast..."

Before he could finish she hacked his head clean off as his body fall to the floor his head flies up and fell to the first floor.

"Nooo! Daddy!" in tears Bella fires at the Empress, but she dodges out of the way and cuts through Bella's right shoulder. So deep the cut she can no longer control her arm. Bella stumbles against the rail and as Empress is about to swing Dragon Bane toward the back of her head Bella is saved by Sunflower blocking the blow.

"This is not over Aj."

"Yes, it is, you already lost Cj." "Now kindly died like a good little girl."

Empress swings Dragon Bane down so hard that Axel can't block it as she drops Sunflower, she reaches for Daisy, Empress slashes her blade across Axel's cutting a large chunk out of her chest, she falls to the floor.

Empress stands over Axel as Bella fires at her using her left hand, Empress spins and drives a dagger deep into Bella's other shoulder causing her to lose control of that arm as well. She stumbles back towards the rail again,

Empress continues cutting and slashing into Bella more and more her upper body lends over the railing Empress grabs her lower body and flips her over it.

Bella lands on the first floor on her back as blood pours from the back of her head agents run to her, but it's already too late.

Trying to stand and reach her sword Axel is intercepted by Dragon Bane as it rakes across her face putting her back on the floor face down.

With her blade against Axel's head, she speaks, "Die Cj, Die." Empress turns and places Dragon Bane right in F's face as he just ran up to her from behind, He raises his hands saying,

"I'm not here to fight. We'll stand down."

She Boast,

"You have seen, what I done here today?"

"Yes."

"All my targets are dead."

"Yes."

"Many of your agents are dead."

"Yes."

"Either I walk out of here peacefully, or more of your agents will die."

F presses his earpiece, "This is F. All agents stand down, I repeat all agents stand down.

Piedmont yells back, "F, you can't give that order you shut the hell up now! All agents move in and take that bitch down!"

As agents start to slowly close in on the Empress F looks around, he presses the piece again, "Look, either she walks out peacefully or more of us will die."

Piedmont interrupts, "Shut up F you fool shut up!"

F continues "We lost enough friends, family, and teammates today, stand down live to fight another day."

The agents put away their weapons and back away opening a path for Empress to walk out, she pulls back her sword and put it away. she leans into F saying, "Good man. You're cute, but if we meet again. I will kill you." She starts walking away, but turns back to him saying, "By the way, she did loved you Mister F. she was just too stubborn to say it." She smiles as she heads off.

F drops to his knees and with tears in his eyes, he grabs Axel, "Cj, Baby girl, Cj."

The Empress walks out, each agent she passes put away their weapon and steps back giving her plenty of room to make her way as they also hear the yelling and bitching of the Colonel ordering them not to let her go.

None of them dare to follow his orders for these agents will go home tonight in one piece, unlike many others that fallen today.

In the large cave in South Korea

Twelve children are knelling, the cave is well-lit, the men above them are watching as the youngsters are meditating. A loud gong rings with a thundering clash! From an opening deeper in the cave out walks The Master.

He has long white hair and long white bread with a connecting mustache. He's flanked on both sides by two of his guardsmen. As he passes each of the children, they each bow their heads without opening their eyes as if they can feel his presence. He sits on a large throne made of stone. He sits back in it to get a good feel of the seat. He looks over his pupils leans forward, and with pride he speaks,

"For 200 years the Jay Clan has taken in youngsters such as yourselves, and we have taught you the ways of the assassin, the warrior, the weapon, the Clan. In each of you, we instilled our beloved code of honor, and our way of life."

As the children open their eyes to place them on their master with undivided attention as he continues,

"You the twelve of twenty-four are the top of this year's class, for your other classmates not here will be full-time stay home members of the Clan. As for you here you have the honor of being sold as weapons to our allies and foes alike."

He stands with his arms stretched upward and looking at the men above he yells to them,

"To the highest bidder goes the spoils!!!"

He points towards the class saying, "Declare yourselves!"

As he begins to fade into darkness, she hears a voice "Cj. Cj. Wake up baby, wake up." She opens her eyes and turns her head toward him sayings, "F? I'm not dead?" He answers, "No baby girl you're not dead." She reacts, "Dam, I was hoping I did not have to explain to you." He questions, "Yes Cj, explain to me. What happened? Who is she? And how do you know her?" She answers,

"Her name is Aj, she's my clan sister." F replies, "Of course. No wonder, she's a Jay just like you." She adds, "Yes, but I thought her to be dead." he replies "Eh, well she sure looked alive yesterday cutting down agents left and right." She replies, "Yesterday?"

She tries to get out of bed but the drugs for pain they gave her won't let her. F gently grabs her saying, "No babe lay back down. You lost a lot of blood." she asks, "Where am I." He tells her, "The infirmary. Easy, lay back down."

Colonel Piedmont burst in yelling, "Is she awake?! Axel! Axel! What the hell happened yesterday?! How in the hell…

F cuts him off "Enough Colonel! She's in no condition for one of your classic tongue lashings! And I'm not gonna stand here and allow you to yell at her, Colonel!

Piedmont answers "You better act gingerly boy. We lost a lot of agents yesterday, not to mention two of our best! So, I want some answers! How the hell did that bitch beat You, Axel?!"

She asks, "Bella, Bella is dead too?" as Piedmont starts to cool down, he answers, "No but she's in ICU and they said it's just a matter of time now, there's nothing they can do."

She looks over to F "I want to see her." F answers, "Baby you can't, you need rest." She repeats "I want to see her F." F looks over at Piedmont, then grabs the phone. Piedmont asks, "What the hell you're doing F?"

Minutes later F is pushing Cj in a wheelchair, they arrive outside Bella's room. He speaks, "Cj they won't let us go in, we can only see her through the window."

As she starts to stand F says, "Babe you need to stay in the chair, you're not strong enough yet." She snaps, "I am fine." She stands and limps towards the window. She sees Bella's broken body in a deep coma. She places her right hand on the glass saying, "I am so sorry I failed you and your father." her eyes close.

She sees Agent Campbell on the floor dead and covered in blood as she hears the voice of Bella saying over and over **"You let my father die. You failed him! You failed him!! You failed him!!!"** His eyes open and reaches up for her. She jumps and opens her eyes as she snaps out of her trance.

F asks her, "Cj, babe are you okay?"

She turns to him saying, "F, I am going home."

He answers, "What?"

She says again, **"I am going home."**

Chapter II

Home Again

The large cave in South Korea

The Master speaks, as he points to the Twelve children, "Declare yourselves!"

The first child speaks she's Fifteen of age, "I Aj am now Dragon Lady, my sword is Dragon's Claw, my dagger is Talon." she bows her head.

The next one speaks he's Sixteen of age, "I Bj am now Striker, my sword is Long Strike, my dagger is Short Strike." he bows.

Next she's Fourteen "I Cj am now Axel, my sword is Sunflower, my dagger is Daisy." she bows.

He's Twelve "I Dj am now Quick Blade, my sword is Cutter, my dagger is Hunter."

The pattern continues as all the other declare themselves to their master, but as the voices begin to fade Darkness looms to what appears to be an old house in the dead of night. Moving down a hallway towards a door at the end, a loud yell and a slash echo from the other side, then a name is screamed **"Cj!!"** the door opens and a young girl's voice yells out **"Dj!!"** a flash of light then darkness.

Her Eyes opens.
At first, she is unaware of her surroundings, but as her head starts to clear, she remembers that she's aboard a flight. She hears a voice saying,

"It's about time you woke up. You've been sleeping ever since we left LA. I was afraid, I wasn't going to get a chance to talk to you, I would really like to get to know you."

She pulls her hood try to cover her face as she tries to pull away from the man, he says,

"Oh, please don't hide your scars they don't bother me. I have scars too. I call them medals."

He extends his hand as he introduces himself,

"Kirk, Kirk Landing." a short pause. He smiles asking, "And you are?" she grabs and shakes his hand answering, "Cj, call me Cj." as she looks into his eyes, she finds herself dropping her guard as she smiles for the first time in a long time.

Jokingly he asks, "So is Korea your vacation, or are you going home?" again she smiles as she answers, "Both."

He replies, "Great maybe you can show me around huh? So what do you do for a living?" she answers,

"I kill people." he pauses, then responds, "Is the pay good?" she laughs, and he smiles saying,

"There you are, I knew you were in there somewhere. So other than killing folks, what else you like to do?"

The two continue talking and laughing throughout the rest of the flight.

A few hours later as the flight is about to land in Seoul, Korea's main airport, she finds herself waking up from the best sleep she's had in some time.

She notices that she was sleeping on Kirk's shoulder the whole time. Somewhat embarrassed she starts to pull back and turn away, but he stops her by placing his hand on her scared cheek and saying,

Hey, hey don't be ashamed, I enjoyed you resting your troubles on my shoulder, you got a good nap in?"

She smiles as she stares into his eyes.

Sometime later outside the airport, Kirk is flagging down a cab. He asks, "Cj will I get to see you again?

She answers, "Yes."

He asks, "What's your contact information, So I can find you."

She answers, "Don't worry, I'll find you." she walks off as he jumps in a cab.

A Few Days Later

A retired US soldier is chopping wood outside his home. As he continues hacking away his only thoughts are of the other tasks, he has waiting for him today. His focus on the wood is broken as he hears a sound coming from the nearby forest.

He looks up and sees something coming out of the woods, he's startled as he drops his ax, and yells out to his wife, who's in the kitchen washing dishes, but can clearly hear and see her husband through a window, and as she looks towards the woodline, she too sees what he's looking at.

She quickly runs toward the front door, once outside she sees that her husband is already embracing their daughter.

With tears in her eyes, she calls out, "Cj! Cj! My baby finally came home."

The father pulls back from Cj so his wife can get her hugs, and kisses in on her baby, then he asks,

"Cj how long have you been living in the forest?"

She answers, "Three days I think."

He asks, "Why, why didn't you just come home? Why did you rough it out there?"

She answers, "I needed a few days to sort some things out Father."

He replies, "Well.." her mother cuts him off saying, "Well you are home now, and we are so happy that you are here." she smiles saying, "Now off to the shower with you."

He agrees, "Yes please do my child off to the shower." they all laugh as they heads toward the house.

Sometime later in the shower, she finds herself mostly just leaning against the wall as the water rains down on her. Her mind is bombarded with thoughts of all her pains and grief, only finding a shimmer of joy when she thinks of the man on the flight,

"He's an older man, 50 something I guess, but I felt so comfortable with him. I don't know, I guess I don't deserve a man like that. I don't deserve any kind of happiness. I am an agent, a killer, an assassin,,, a murderer."

Her mind pauses for a bit before she asks herself, *"I wonder what F is doing now."*

Meanwhile back in the States, in Colonel Piedmont's office, F finds himself in the middle of a heated debate, well argument with the Colonel.

"Well F?
"Well, what colonel?"
"Don't play games with me F. Where the hell is she?"
"Cj went home Colonel."
"Home? Home!! Are you kidding me F?!"
"No, I'm not sir. She went home, back to Korea."
"And you let her go without you?"
"Obviously Colonel."
"And they say you're the smart one, F you're a fool. A lovesick puppy ass fool."
"The hell with you,,, colonel."

"No, the hell with you boy. You allow one of our deadliest weapons to leave from out of our umbrella of control, and to do what? Find herself? F, you're a sentimental fool, and the killer part is she doesn't even love you. Boy, you're something else."

F slams both his hands on Piedmont's desk.

"Enough, Colonel! She wanted to go alone, and not me, you or your whole dam division could've stopped her, and you know it. So do yourself a favor, and get off my back, and for the record sir… You can kiss my ass three ways from Sunday."

"How dare you talk to me like that boy."

F leaves the office saying,

"I dare Colonel. If you want your weapon back so bad, then you go and bring her back against her will. Good luck with that."

F slams the door as Piedmont stands up, *"That arrogant son of a bitch, I run this division, I'll show him and his psycho killing bitch. I'll show them all!"*

Back in Korea

Cj is sitting down to have dinner with her parents. For the first few minutes, all is quiet until the silence is broken by her father, "So, have you visited your Master yet?"

Cj answers, "No, not yet." he doubles down, "But you are planning on seeing him, right?" she responds, "I wish not to talk about that right now."

He stops eating as he asks, "You haven't forgiven us, have you?" she starts to answer but her mother cuts her off,

"Of course she has, or she would not be here,,, right?" Cj stands up and says, "You asked if I forgive you for what you had done to me. I don't hold it against you because it is clear you have not forgiven yourselves. I can not put the time, nor the energy into your pain and grief. I have my own demons to fight."

She walks away as her father reaches for her mother's hand. Once their hands embraces, her mother cries.

Late that night Cj walks down the hallway, she sees a door at the end. She heads towards it. She reaches for the knob to open it, but it springs open on its own. She sees Capricorn standing there. Cj speaks, "Capri,,, hey it's me, Axel. Capricorn doesn't respond. Just as Cj is about to speak again, Capricorn starts talking, but no sound is heard from her mouth. Cj reacts, "What, what are you saying I cannot hear you." She sees that Capricorn's mouth is moving faster, and faster, but still no sound. "What, I cannot hear you, Capri." She notices that Capricorn's lips appear to be only saying one word over and over. "I cannot hear,,, I do not understand." Capricorn's head starts to move side to side in rhythm with her mouth movement, her eyes start to turn jet black, and her skin turns pale like a corpse. An icy chill runs down Cj's back as fear begins to grip her. Capricorn suddenly stops… She lets out a thundering demon-like growl, **"Murderer!!!"**

Cj wakes up from her nightmare. Her eyes are full of tears. She sits up against the headboard of the bed. She pulls her legs toward her chest, and lays her head on her knees whimpering,

"F, I need you." she cries.

Meanwhile, back in the states, F is lying in bed with the sheets only covering his lower half. He's unable to sleep. He's stuck staring at the ceiling, with tears running down his face. He knows that Cj needs him, but she's so far away, and there's nothing he can do about it. All he can think of is,

"I should have gone with her, I should have found a way to convince her to let me go with her."

For him this is every night since she's been gone.

Morning back in Korea

An old man is tending his garden at his nice but modest home. As he enjoys his labor, he notices he's visited by a past student of his

"Hello, Master."
"Cj my little warrior has returned, or should I call you Axel now?"
"What happened to the temple Master? What happened to the order?"
"My young student, the Jay Clan is no more, but I've heard, of your great works Young One."
"What is great about killing, Master?"

"More than you know to understand Young One. Many men and women are known to be great in history simply by the people they have killed. Kings, queens, warriors, soldiers, lawmen, presidents, and robbers are mostly known for whom they killed, then what they built. A wave of death is the legacy of many of the greats of our history, Young One."

"But Master."

He looks deeply into her eyes saying, "Ah, eh, Haha... You're having the nightmares uh?"

"Yes, but how, how did you know about my…?"

"Ah, I would not be much of a teacher if I didn't know about the nightmares. They are the curse that the clan must endure."

"But why Master, why must we all suffer such torment?"

"Ah, because Young One, one kill is an accident, two kills, is a mistake, ah but kill three, four, five, and so on. Then it is clear what you truly are, and the nightmares will not let you forget that. It is the way of the Clan, it is the way of all killers, it's what separates the men from the beast."

"For someone whose conscience does not torment that person, then he's truly a monster among men."

And you Master? Do the nightmares haunt you as well?

"No, my child, not I. Ever the teacher of killers, never a killer myself. So, for me to know of them comes from our Clan's old writings and the words of many of my past students."

"Fear not Young One you can control your pasted demons, by defeating your present ones."

"One that has bested you at every turn, one that you know in your heart that you must kill or be killed by…"

"Aj, you are speaking of Aj"

"Yes, my child, you must defeat her. This is the only way to ease some of your torment. I see you are not sure if you can beat her. Come back here tomorrow and we will begin your training, your advanced training."

"Yes, Master. Thank you."

A few hours later at the local market, Cj is with her parents.

"How did I let them talk me into coming here? People buying, selling, and haggling over prices for food, clothes, and other goods, and services. To the untrained mind all this would seem like utter chaos." On the other hand, there is a harmony in this organized mess of people, Uh..."

Her thoughts are interrupted when she bumps into someone, "Oh excuse me... You,,, Kirk." with excitement Kirk replies,

"Cj, I finally found you." she responds, "What?" he explains, "I figured a young lady like you wouldn't live in the big city, so I started searching the nearby villages and I finally caught up with you."

"Really Kirk, you think you caught your prey."

"I didn't mean it like that Cj. What I meant was..."

"I know what you meant Kirk."

"I bet that's the first time you've smiled since our flight."

"Yes, it is. What do you want from me, Kirk?"

"Well, we can start with dinner and a few drinks, then maybe later get lucky."

"After you get lucky, then what Kirk?"

"Uh, I don't know Cj,,, a ring, house, two maybe three kids."

"That sounds like marriage Kirk."

"Well. How about it?"

"You would have me, Kirk?"

"Yeah. Why not?"

"I've told you. I kill people for a living."

"Well, we all have our faults."

She smiles.

Two Days Later in her Master's Backyard

Cj is on her second day of intense physical training, and swordsmanship. As she works her way from one drill or task to another her Master speaks to her,

"A lion roars, a tiger growls, an elephant stomps, an eagle soars, and a caterpillar transforms. All animals have their own powers, skills, weapons, and defense…"

"You, My young student, have your own as well, but now the time has come for you to elevate to a higher level and find your new power, skill, weapon, and defense.

Aj is my greatest student, and in order to best her you must elevate beyond her level, like no other ever has." She almost killed you the last time you faced off. You must remove the fears of that moment in order to advance, grow, evolve."

She stops her workout, stands to face him, and asks,

"Master, how do you know of my last encounter with her?"

He answers, "Young One, I keep up with the comings and goings of all my students. I would not be much of a teacher if I did not." Go now much rest you need. Tomorrow young one."

she replies, "Tomorrow Master." she leaves.

Chapter III
Laying Nightmares to Rest

Inside the Large Cave, somewhere in South Korea what seems like Ages Ago to some.

Early before the young ones declare themselves to the Clan's leader, the top four of the Twelve are preparing for the ceremony. Little Dj walks up to Cj, grabs her hand saying,

"Cj I do not want to do this, I do not want us to be separated."

Cj responds, "I'm sorry Dj, but it is what we are trained for. We must do as the Clan does, it is our way."

Dj asks, "But, but who's going to sing to me, or tell me stories so I can sleep at night?"

Cj answers, "I do not know little one, I do not know."

Dj drops his head admitting, "Really going to miss you, Cj."

She looks down at him smiling, "Me too little one, me too.

Aj steps over to them saying, "You baby him too much Cj."

Cj responds, "So what?"

Aj answers, "So what? He's about to be a full member of the Jay Clan. An honored warrior, an honored assassin, an..."

Bj interrupts, "A killer, a murderer, an evil weapon to be used at others' discretion."

Aj reacts, "Hold your tongue, Bj."

He replies, "Why should I? It is the truth. Each of our parents sold us to the Clan at the age of four. And the Clan raised us to be world-class assassins, to be sold off again to the highest bidder."

She answers, "It is our way, it is the way of the clan."

He replies, "It is a lost way, an evil way of blood and death."

She demands, "You will, you must declare yourself to the Clan, or you will be killed Bj… Bj?"

He responds, "Do not worry about me Aj, I am too well trained not to do as I was trained for,"

A tear starts to run down Dj's face.

Bj smiles and rubs the top of Dj's head saying, "Do not fear little one, all will be well." Dj smiles.

Ej adds, "Yeah, we are going to kick ass when we move on to our new homes and the world with fear the Clan, they will fear us."

Just then a loud gong sounds a Clan member walks in saying, "It is time young one."

She stretches her arm out showing the way as all twelve kids heads for the main chamber of the cave.

Sometime later after all the kids have declared themselves to the clan, the Master stands up faces his students and proudly bows to them, he looks up towards their military guest on the balcony and announces,

"Let the binding begin!!"

Moving down a hallway towards a door at the end, a loud yell and a slash echo from the other side, then a name is screamed **"Cj!!"** the door opens and a young Aj's voice yells out **"You can't save him Cj, you can't stop me, Cj!!"** A loud voice yells **Dj!!"** a flash of light... then darkness.

Her Eyes opens

She lets go a loud scream. Hearing her scream in the next room her mother jumps out of bed to rush to her. Her father grabs her mother's hand saying,

"No remember what she said, no matter what we hear she said not to come in her room."

"But papa she needs us."

"No mama if we do not do as she asked, we might push her away forever."

The parents sat on the bed unable to go back to sleep. The mother cries as the father tries to comfort her.

The next day
After another intense workout, Cj asks her Master, "Master, tell me please… What happened to Bj, why do I keep seeing him in my nightmares?"

He answers, "Young one, you know what happened to him, you were there… Oh, oh Haha…" he places his finger against her temple as he continues, "Over the course of time you have forced you mind to forget, and suppress the events of that day… This is how you have chosen to fight your demons is it? My student this is not the best way to combat them… To remove memories from yourself will cause you many holes in your mind, this will lead to you one day losing yourself completely… The best way to combat your demons is to face them head-on Young One…

"Go back, go back, go back to that day, and remember, remember..." He continues to chant as her mind begins to **Flashback** to that day………..

The cave. Aj has just finished displaying her combat skills and has sit back down with the other kids.

The Master looks up to see the men binding for the young assassin. A signal is made the Master speaks.

"The binding is over. Aj the Dragon Lady now belongs to the Unknown Agency,,, The UA. Aj declare yourself." Aj stands, she bows to her old master she bows to her new ones, "I declare myself to the UA!"

The Master orders, "Bj the Striker display your combat skills to the bidders."

Bj stands up he starts to walk toward the ring as he thinks,

"I do not want this, I do not want this." he whispers, "I do not want this, I do not want this." His voice gets louder and louder as he steps into the middle of the ring. He yells out! "I, Do not,,, Want this!!!"

He runs heading for the cave's exit. The Master smiles as if he knew the young ′man would run, for this is nothing new to the Clan for in every class there's always a runner. He orders,

"Aj bring him back please." She rises replying, "Yes master." she chases after Bj.

About ten minutes later the Master orders, "Cj bring them both back please."

She replies, "Yes Master." as she follows them.

Minutes later Cj catches up with them, she sees them sword-fighting by the edge of a cliff. She tries to intervene but she's too late as she watches Aj ram her sword into Bj's cheat. Still standing as the life starts to fade from his body, Aj kicks him off the edge to his death.

Cj yells his name as she charges Aj who uses Cj's momentum against herself, forcing her off the cliff, but Cj is close

enough to the edge to grab it and hold
on for dear life.

Aj stands over Cj who fighting to hold on to the ledge, "He was weak Cj, and you are weak, but Dj is the weakest of all. I will cleanse the Clan of you all. I'm not going to kill you now, I want you to feel the pain of the death of your little boyfriend Dj."

Cj yells "Do not touch him! Do not touch him'!!" Aj smiles as she walks away. "Do not touch him!!!"

The flashback is over, but her Master continues to chant as she falls into another flashback...

The hallway, the door at the end a loud yell **"Cj nooooo!"** the door opens. Cj is holding Dj who's mortally wounded.

She's begging him not to die as Aj stands over them laughing. "Please, Dj please don't die." but he has no choice in the matter. As life fades from his body Cj begins to cry.

Aj speaks, "Like I said,,, weak. Now both are dead, and you could not save them from me. I will not kill you Cj, no I want you to suffer the pain of knowing that every man who shows any love toward you will be my target and you will never find love, or happiness, cause if you do, I will hunt you down and rip out your heart again and again until you die. And there is nothing you can do to stop me because you cannot defeat me. Haha yes, I am your living demon that will haunt you from here to forever." "From here to forever." Aj fades into the darkness as Cj screams her name "AaaaJjjj!!!"

She snaps out of her trance as her Master stops chanting. "Aj,,, Aj is my Demon that haunts my dreams?"

The master answers, "Yes my young student."

"And I must defeat her to be rid of her taunting and haunting of my very being?"

"Again, yes my young student."

"Then I will face her head on Master, I will kill her"

"Yes Young One, but be warned. In order to defeat her you must rise to a higher level, you must lose yourself to move yourself above her."

She pauses to ponder his words.

He continues, "From here you go, come back no more, learned all I have to teach you Young One." As he heads for the front door of his humble home she says to him,

"Goodbye, my Master."

Later that evening

Cj sits with her parents at dinner when her mother notices, "You have not touched your food, Cj."

"I cannot eat tonight Mother."

Her father asks, "More of your master's training huh?"

She answers, "No Father."

Her mother asks, "Are you planning another date with that nice black American,,, what's his name eh, oh yes, Kirk, is it?

"No Mother, Kirk and I can never be together. I cannot be with anyone, not while I have battles to fight."

Her father asks, "So, you're going to fight her again huh?"

Shocked she asks, "How do you know about..."

He cuts her off, "About your fight with Aj back in the states?"

Again she asks, "How do you know?"

He answers, "You forget I am an ex-US soldier, an officer. I may live here with your mother, but I still have my military contacts stateside, and I have been following your career as a Jay Clan Assassin. I know every mission you've been on, everyone you killed, even the ones you failed to protect. Yes, Cj I knew Agent Campbell, we played football together back at West Point. He was,,, he was a good friend."

More shocked she asks, "When he came to me, did he know about me? Did he know I am your daughter?"

He answers, "Yes, I told him everything about you and your connection with Aj the Empress. It was I that convinced him you could defeat her. I am sorry, I did not know you were not ready for her."

Angrily she stands up saying, "I am ready for her now!"

As she is leaving, her mother yells, "No! Baby, please do not go!" her father grabs her mother's hand saying, "No, she must go, she must do this. There is nothing we can do." As he holds her in his arms she cries.

Moments later Cj is sitting on her bed. Her mind starts to wonder about her fears and pain. But suddenly her mind drifts toward something more pleasant. Her date with Kirk, the thoughts of that day and night brings her to smile.

First a tour of the town,

"You going to show me your hometown
Cj?"

"I have been away for a long time, you
probably know more about the town
than I do.

Let's explore it together."

Next a matinee movie.

A wonderful movie of love and romance,
and nobody dies.

"Did you enjoy the movie, Cj?"

"Yes, it was amazing Kirk."

Then dinner at a nice eatery.

"What would you like to eat Cj?"

"I will let you pick Kirk, I trust you."

Finally, a walk on the beach with a beautiful moonlight.

"So, tell me Cj have I earned a second date?"

"Yes, Kirk you have definitely earned a second date."

"The moonlight sparkle in your eyes, it so beautiful Cj, you're so beautiful."

The silence of two staring into each other's eyes, the invisible force pulling them closer to each other the pressing

together of their lips or as we humans
say the kiss.

She snaps out of her trance, she notices
a note on her dresser she hasn't seen
before, she goes over grabs and reads
it.

Hello Cj/Axel
why have you not come to see me by
now,
I have been waiting for you.
Come, come see me, Axel,
you know where to find me.
Your Living Demon.
PS,
I know about your new man.

"Aj,,, I will come see you bitch, I will kill you." She grabs her blades and leaves.

Near-by the Old Cliff

Aj has a camp set up and it appears that she's been there for days waiting. She steps out of her tent and starts to tend the campfire,

"What is taking her so long I waited all night for her."

She hears that someone is now behind her, she speaks,

"It is about time you got here Cj, what took you so long?"

Cj responds, "It just so happens that you are here in Korean when I am huh? How convenient it is right?"

Aj replies, "That is how our story is written Cj, we are both just pieces on a chessboard except I am a bishop, knight, and rook all rolled into one, while you are just a plain old everyday pawn, so you do know how our story will end right.?

        "Stand and face me, Aj."

Aj stands to face her foe, as Cj continues, "It is I that will edition our story with your death, you have much to pay for."

"Me?! No Cj you owe me blood bitch!"

"The only thing I owe you Aj is the tips of Sunflower."

Cj draws her sword and gives Aj the universal swordsman's salute, Aj draws her blade and returns the salute. The showdown is now officially underway as the two sides step to get a feel for one another.

Aj taunts "I see the fear in your eyes." Cj charges their sword clash "TING" They clash again, again, and again, their swords lock as they come close face to face.

Aj can now see the determination in Cj's eyes, *"I need room."* she thinks as she headbutts Cj who falls back, but she quickly recovers as she legs sweep Aj off her feet.

Cj swings downward on Aj but she keeps rolling and dodging each time, but she notices, *"Her reaction time has gotten better."* she yells out as Cj's sword drives through her thigh "You bitch!"

She draws her digger and throws it toward Cj's head causing her to dodge which gives Aj room and time to get back to her feet. Blood gushing for her leg causing her to feel weak. "You gotten stronger, Master taught you well Cj."

Cj charges and swings her sword down as hard as she can, Aj blocks, Cj swings again, again and again Aj continues to block, but each blow gets stronger and stronger harder, and harder to block, taking more and more out of her. She also losing ground pushing her back to the edge of the cliff.

Cj stops as Aj sticks her sword into the ground and raises her hands as if, she's asking for a time-out or pause in the fight.

Cj lowers her blade as Aj begins to speak, "You see you cannot kill me, you will not do it, for you do not have the..." she is interrupted by Sunflower slicing her throat taking a large chunk from her neck, before she could react Cj follows by ramming Sunflower into Aj's cheat.

Aj tried to speak but could not. Cj kicks Aj off the cliff as she pulls her blade out of her.

Falling to her death Aj thinks, *"I do not believe it, the bitch killed me!"* As she continues falling to her death the last thing, she sees is Cj standing at the cliff's edge in victory.

Cj watches her living Demon fall for good.

She smiles.

Chapter IV
A New Dream

Korea eighteen years ago

A four-year-old girl is sold by her parents to the Jay Clan of Assassins. She was heartbroken, she felt thrown away, an outcast, abandoned. This was her first demon.

She was introduced to her Master teacher, she will have many other teachers and instructors, but he's the Master of the Clan. The Clan named her Cj.

She meets six-year-old Aj who was mean to her from the start. This was her main demon.

She meets seven-year-old Bj, he protects her from Aj, he makes her feel welcome when others wouldn't.

At the age of six, she meets four-year-old little Dj, she takes him under her wing like a big sister singing to him and comforting him on his first night away from his parents. It was the first time she ever tried to sing. He loved it.

At the age of eight, it was time to make her first kill. The Clan caught a rouge crime lord, and she was tasked to execute him. Not wanting to do it, her teachers told her she must, or she would never see Dj again.

She grabs the sword, it's very heavy for an eight-year-old's hand, but she manages to raise it as high as she could. As Clan member held down the rouge, she sliced the sword down across his neck. He yells out of fear not of pain as the sword didn't cut him, it shattered in her hand it was a fake.

The Clan wanted to see if she would be willing to kill and she passed her test. All clan members must take this test at age eight.

At age ten she watched eight-year-old Dj take the test. He only did it because they told him he couldn't see her anymore.

At age twelve she starts to have fantasies of being happily married with children of her own. She starts to believe that little Dj will grow to be her man someday.

She starts to see him not as a little brother anymore but as her future soulmate, which did lead to some awkward times.

She's twelve now this is the age when Clan members have to get their first kill for real. This time when she faced the rouge crime lord she didn't hasted, she sliced his head clean off.

Her first steps of becoming a killing machine, and yet another creation of a demon she must battle over the years.

At the age of fourteen moment before their declaring ceremony. As she holds Dj's hand she looks down and stare into his eyes, she tells him,

"Dj, you are the only thing in this world that I truly love."

He replies, "I love you too Cj." she pauses as he smiles,

"No Dj, I mean I truly love you. You stole my heart long ago. When you grow into manhood, I know deep in my heart we will be together, and when you are older you will understand the words I am saying to you now. No matter what happens, no matter how far they separate us, we will be together.

A tear flows down his cheeks, she kisses him. He's in stock. For the first time in his young life, he's in love. His childhood crush he didn't know he had, has manifested itself right before his eyes. (Amazing What Can Just Fall Right into Your Lap Unexpectedly).

Just in front of them, both Bj and Aj heard all that was said. Bj smiles because he sees it as another reason why they should not be forced into the life of killing whomever their soon-to-be new paymasters want dead.

On the other hand, the whole thing sickens Aj to her very core, since she first set her eyes on Cj she hated her.

At year six she meets Cj for the first time, "What is your name? Cj huh? Well, I do not like you Cj." tears in her eyes little Cj asks, "Why?" Aj replies, "Because you are ugly and weak."

At eight years old after her willingness to kill test, she would tease Cj by telling and showing her the many different ways she could kill her. Cj had many sleepless nights until finally, Bj put a stop to it, "Aj stop your taunting of Cj, or I will take you to the Master myself and he will punish you for your attacks."

At the age of ten, she punched Cj repeatedly over a joke about her that Cj did not even tell, but she thought it was funny. The sight and sounds of Cj laughing at her caused her to blow up, never mind that others were laughing even harder at her, but her revenge sights were totally on Cj, as she introduced her fist to Cj's face many times before Bj could grab and pull her off, "Dam you Aj why you jumped Cj? It was Ej who told the joke, why you do not attack him?

Ej responds, "She best not. She picked the weakest of us."

Aj answers, "Her weakness sickens me!" she storms off as Dj tries to comfort Cj as she cries.

At age Twelve during one of so many sword training matches over time Cj finally bested Aj by disarming her. Cj never felt so proud. But it was short-lived as Aj drew her dagger and threw it at the unsuspecting Cj, it pierced into her shoulder, Cj yelled out in pain crying,

"Why!? Why!? Why!?" As the trainer tends to Cj, the Master witnessed the entire event, He came down. He steps to Aj, and with anger he has not displayed since his youth, he slaps the taste from her mouth.

(Since that day everything she eats, taste like the palm of his hand) She couldn't even stand back up, Clan members had to drag her to her room.

At age Fifteen just after hearing how much Cj loves Dj, Aj thinks. *"So, she loves him. From here on I will kill every man she loves, she will never know love, she will never have peace… This I vow."* Cj looks at her as if she could hear what Aj was thinking."

Cj eyes open as Kirk says, "It's about time you woke up. You've been sleeping since we left Seoul, we're about to land in LA now."

"I have been sleeping that long?"

"Yeah girl, you must really be tired. Some vacation huh?"

Later after they claimed their bags He says, "Well LA is my stop. What about you where are you heading to? She answers,

"I was hoping I could stay at your place."

He responds, "With me? Really?"

she answers, "Yes really."

He asks, "For how long?"

She replies, "For as long as you want me."

He yells, "Yes!" as he picks her up spins her around then stops. They kiss as some people in the airport clap.

A few weeks pass as she and Kirk spend time together, dinner, movies, days on the beach, and quiet nights cuddling at a cozy fire. She has never been happier. She hasn't had a nightmare since she moved in with him. She feels herself healed from the scars of her passed. Now she feels finally free to love and be loved.

While relaxing on the couch she asks him, "Why have you not asked me to marry you Kirk?"

he answers, "I didn't want to pressure you, I'm waiting for you to be ready."

She smiles passionately saying, "Ask me."

"Cj, will you marry me?"

She smiles like never before saying, "Yes Kirk, I will."

They Kiss.

Later that night she wraps both her sword and dagger in cloth, zips them in a black bag, and sets them in a hole in Kirk's backyard behind a shed,

"I pray I never again have to use you two. Sleep well." she covers them with the dirt along with daisy and sunflower seeds.

Back at the Agency
in F's Office/Laboratory

F is talking with the agent known as Axel Grease Monkey aka, Mister Fix-It-All.
"F, How did the Blue-light device work for you?"
"It works like a charm Greasy. I it was earlier to patch up Cj's injuries since you made it."
"Great F, you got anymore ideas you want me to build for you?"

"No, but I need you to improve on the inter workings of our basic jamming devices."
"Oh, those things. I'll check them out this weekend for you F."

Just then Colonel Piedmont storms into F's office enraged, "F!"

F jump up from his chair, "Hold the hell up Colonel, you can't just bomb rush in here yelling at me like I'm your child. You best check yourself."

Piedmont responds "Haha, check myself? Haha, you better check your girl, simp."

Both F and Piedmont looks over at Grease Monkey. He starts to feel like he's at the wrong place at the wrong time, "Hey, uh look I'll be going now and let you guys work things out." Piedmont yells, "Yes Grease Monkey you do that!" Just before he walks out the door he says, "Oh and F I'll take care of that for you. Catch you later." He leaves.

F asks, Piedmont "Calmed down yet?" Piedmont answers "No, have you?" as he drops photos on F's desk. He continues, "Guess what your girl has been doing."

After seeing some of them, F is shocked, but tries to hide it saying, "She's not my girl colonel."

Don't lie to me F, I know you and Axel had a thing going."

"That thing we had been over for a while, and it's none of your business… Colonel."

"What is my business F is one of my agents who has been off the grid for some time on leave and hasn't once checked in. She came back to the States and didn't make any contact with home base. Is she gone rogue or what?"

"She's not gone rogue colonel."

"Then I need you to get to LA, go to the house of this guy Kirk Landing, and bring agent Axel back into the fold, and I mean right now F.”

“We can’t,,, I can’t make her come back, she’ll come back when she’s ready.”

“Well, you better try, and I mean hurry she’s about to be married soon.”

“WHAT!!!”

“Yesss F, in a few days she’ll be Mrs. Landing. Uh, you didn’t know?”

“Of course, I didn’t know. How the hell do you know all this?”

“F, your mind does go blank when it comes to her. You know good and well we have agents everywhere. She was spotted as soon as her flight landed weeks ago."

F sits back down in her chair as Piedmont continues, "Look F I understand that you have much love for her, but you've got to understand, she's not a woman, not a wife or future mother, she's a weapon, a killing machine nothing more than that. Once you realize that, then maybe you can take your heart out of her hand, and pull your head out of her ass, then maybe we can all get back to protecting this country like we're supposed to be doing."

Piedmont heads for the door, he stops saying, "Go to LA and talk her into coming back to work. That's an order agent. Because if I have to get involved it's will to get messy."

F finally responds, "If it gets messy,,, she will make you pay. Believe that Colonel."

Piedmont replies, "We'll see agent, we'll see. Now get going." he leaves the room.

F looks at the photos, then rakes them all off his desk. He places his face in his hands saying, "Dam, dam, dam."

Two Days later, Los Angeles

The doorbell rings, the door is answered by Kirk who says, "Hello can I help you." before the visitor can speak, he hears her voice as she comes to the door, "Who is it baby?" smiling and hugging on Kirk she looks and sees,

"F, hey how are you?" he tries to smile as he answers, "Cj, I'm good. It's good to see you."

He starts to leave until she says, "Wait F." she turns to Kirk saying, "Baby let me talk to him in private please." he answers, "Sure babe." he kisses her, then addresses F, "So you're F? I heard a lot about you." he nods his head as a sign of respect, F returns the gesture as Kirk walks away.

Cj steps outside closing the door behind her, "F, I..."

He cuts her off "It's okay Cj, as long as you're happy I'm happy." It's good to see you smile again. I guess you found what you were looking for." I'm sorry to be the bringer of bad news, but the Colonel wants you back in action, but I can see you're not even thinking about coming back are you?"

She drops her head saying, "No, I do not want that life anymore. I am tired of killing."

He replies, "I figured that much. Look at me Cj. I want you to continue to be happy and enjoy your new life. But you know as I do, the Agency is everywhere and Piedmont is determined to bring you back by any means necessary. Watch yourself, and your man Cj."

As he's about to leave she hugs and kisses him on the cheek, he hugs her rubbing his hand on her bottom and whispering in her ear, they break their embrace as he says,

"Goodbye Cj." she replies as he walks away "Goodbye F."

She watch him get into his car and drives away, she waves.

In a window, Kirk seen the whole thing.
He thinks

"Well, that was intense."

Twenty minutes later F walks into his hotel room he's shocked to see Piedmont sitting in the chair by the desk he thinks to himself,

"This dude."

He asks,
"Why you're in my hotel room Colonel?"

"You know why I'm here F. How did it go? Is she coming back?"

"I Don't think she's coming back Colonel, and we can't make her."

Piedmont stands up while saying, "Alright F you had your chance, now it's my turn."

F asks, "What,,, You're going to do colonel?" Piedmont doesn't answer as he heads for the door. F yells, "What you're gonna do!?"

Piedmont replies, "Next time I send you on a mission, get a better hotel to stay in, hell son I know we pay you better than this dump." He leaves slamming the door laughing."

Outside Piedmont walks toward his limo halfway to it he walks up to three agents in black suits, and shades. He address them,

"Things just got messy. Bring him."

The agents walks towards F room as Piedmont gets in the back seat of the limo, grabs his car phone dials, speaking,

"Yes, execute plan B., and bring that bitch back home."

Meanwhile in F's room he notices that the Colonel carved something on the desk, "That son of a bitch." The door bursts open.

Earlier

Just after F drives away, Cj waves till she can no longer see him. She thinks,

"I am so sorry that I hurt you F."

Kirk steps outside, he stands behind her asking, "Baby are you alright?"

She turns and smiles at him saying, "What F and I had is long gone, It's about you and me now baby."

He says, "We need to talk baby."

"Please Kirk, I do not want to talk about the Agency's stuff right now."

He asks, "You're sure?" She answers smiling, "One hundred percent baby, one hundred percent." they hug, and kiss.

Moving down a hallway

She walking towards a door at the end, a loud yell and a gunshot echo from the other side, a scream **"Cj!!"** the door opens Kirk standing there with a bullet hole in his forehead, he reaches for her saying, "Nooooo!"

Her eyes open,
Her mind wonders, *"Something wrong."*
She starts to get out of bed, but first,
she tries to remove Kirk's arms from

being wrapped around her without waking him.

"You're okay Cj?"
"Kirk hush, something wrong."
He asks, "What is it baby?"
She replies, "Someone's in the house."

He unwraps his arms from her, and she eases out of bed and tips to the door, placing her head against it. She turns to Kirk, "Get dressed now." he gets out of bed and grabs a pair of pants and shoes.

"Cj we need to talk."
"Not now Kirk."

She put on some shorts and a tee shirt, she headed for the door saying,

"Stay here."

He tried to speak to her "Cj waits." it was too late she left closing the door behind her. He thinks,

"Dam it, this is not supposed to be happening."

He reaches under the bedpost, pressing a button that opens a secret panel where he has a rack of rifles and boxes of ammo.

Meanwhile, Cj's creeping downstairs barefooted so she can sneak up to whomever may be in the house.

She sees,

"Red target lights,,, Gunmen… Humm, Six maybe seven of them."

Back in the room, Kirk has just loaded a rifle, he turns and sees,

"You, what are you doing here? This was not the plan."

Moments later a gunshot is heard from the room, she hears it, "Kirk!!!!" she runs back toward the bedroom yelling his name as the gunmen shots at her missing terribly.

She enters the room, seeing only Kirk's dead body on the bed she runs over to him, "No no no no! Kirk! Kirk!

She cries as she holds him in her arms, his blood covers her face and clothes. She continues to hold him until she hears,

"Gunmen in the hallway."

She looking around. On the floor she sees, "A rifle? Where did it come fr,,, No matter."

She jumps down grabbing it as she rolls away from the bed, she points it toward the door as two goons enter. She blasts them and continues to fire until it locks.

In the hallway, the other goons return fire unloading till all must reload.

An eerie silence reeks from the bedroom, the men cautiously enters. They only see the dead man Kirk on the bed and their two teammates who tried to enter earlier dead on the floor.

The head goon orders, "Shake the place down she got to be here somewhere fan-out."

One of the Goons yells, "Look the window's opened he and the leader see Cj running throw the yard, the goon raises his weapon to fire, but the leader stops him,

"Forget it she's long gone."
                    "But she shot Jimmy."

"I said forget it!"
        another goon asks, "What do we do
                                now."

"We follow our orders, touch the place, and get the hell out of here... Besides she's bleeding." he continues as he rubs some of her blood off the window ledge "She won't get too far."

Chapter V
Revenge Unsweetened

Moving down a hallway towards a door at the end, a loud yell and a slash echo from the other side, out walks Bj who hand gestures for her to go in, but she refuses. Another yell and slash of a blade, Dj walks out, he gestures for her to go in again she refuses. The sound of someone being stabbed, Capricorn and Bart Campbell walks out they too offer Cj to go in, once again she refuses. A gunshot, Kirk walks out, and goes over to Cj gently grabs her hand and leads her to the door, and places her hand on the doorknob, she yells "No I do not want to go in, please do not make me. A flash of bright light…

Her Eyes opens
She wakes up on a park bench, she can see from a distance that there's been a house fire, in her heart she knows whose house it is.

She checks the watch she took from Kirk's dead wrist before she jumped out of the window earlier.

"It is just 2am, I have only been sleeping for an hour and a half. Ouch, my leg. Forgot I got shot back in the room. I need to change the tourniquets."

She rips another piece from her shirt, unwraps the old bloody cloth from her wound, and wraps a new tourniquet to slow down the bleeding. She heads back to the house.

Minutes later she hides until the last of the firemen, police, news, and neighbors leave the scene. She walks up to the burned-down house that was to be her happy new home, now just smoldering piles of ash. She thinks,

"I going to kill that son of a,,, F? I need to find F. Wait, he rubbed my butt earlier." she reaches into the back pocket of her shorts, "F slipped this business card in my pocket, that slick bastard. The Daggot Hotel, on the back

of it, the number 44 must be his room number. He also whispered something to me too, what was it."

She thinks for a bit then she remembers in a flashback, "Under the bed Cj, under the bed."

She can see through the rubble that the shed in the backyard is still standing untouched. She heads for it. She stands over where her blades are buried,

"Sunflower, Daisy, I need you both now more than ever. Wait the ground has been tampered with."

She digs, until she sees the sword bag, but also finds a box with a letter taped on top of it in the hole as well. She removes the letter and reads it...

Dear Cj,
First, I want to tell you how much I
love you and how much I want to
keep you safe, if
you are reading this it must not only
mean that
the bad guys got me, it's also means
that
you feel the need to avenge me, but
let me ask, beg you to go another
way.
Inside the bag are untraceable
money, credit cards, and gold bars
all totaling 60 million dollars.

I'm begging you to forget getting even, take the money and run, disappear, get off the grid, and start a new life and live happily ever after, and if you do now want to do this alone, then I ask you to take F with you and be happy, I know he will do a better job protecting you than I ever could. But if you still feel that you cannot let it go and you must get them bastards, there is a bag under the flood in the shed that is full of what you need to get the job done.
I Love you
always and forever
Kirk

Tears fall from her eyes as she grabs the box and blades. She steps into the shed and notices the loose floor panels, she removes them and grabs the bag she opens it, *"Yes I can use all of this here."* She sees a note she reads it.

Okay you pick the revenge route, you know who killed me so go get that son of a bitch, As you may know by now, yes I was an agent for the agency, I have been trying to tell you but could never find the right time, plus I feared losing you. I should have trusted you more, please forgive me Cj
Love you so much,
Kirk

With more tears flowing from her eyes she grabs both bags and the box, she throws them in the back of Kirk's car and hot-wires it, diving off.

Daggot Hotel room 44

After picking the lock she walks in and immediately notices, *"There been a struggle, a fight. They got him."*

She sees that someone carved words on the desk, she reads it,

You can still save him,
C.P.

"Colonel Piedmont, that bastard."

She looks under the bed and finds a gift F left for her.

"A control jamming device, with all the security codes programmed in. Thanks, F this is going to make things easier."

She also notices, *"F's Blue-light device. I can use this so I can remove the bullet from my leg and stitch up the wound."*

Sometime later after tending her injury she lays on the bed and ponders the letters Kirk wrote her, she thinks,

"Maybe I should just take the money and run… But knowing that F's life is in danger,,, well I could not live with myself. That would be the worst demon

of them all." Just then she drifts into a deep sleep.

The hallway, the door, Bj, Dj, Capricorn, Campbell, and Kirk all pointing toward it wanting her to go in. "No no no I do not want to go in!" They all stare at her angrily, she says again, "I do not want to go in!!" They all scream at her saying, **"You must Cj, you will Cj!!!"** A flash of bright light.

Her eyes opens
She sits up saying out loud, "My name is **AXEL!"**

She jumps out of bed, moment later she's in the bathroom finally washing off Kirk's blood from her hands and face.

She reaches into Kirk's bag and pulls out a black spandex one-piece combat suit, she puts it on, she strips on her sword belt and a gun belt, *"Guns, I really do not care for them, but I have to even the field."*

Now completely armed and ready to rumble she grabs the jamming device, the blue-light device, and bags, she heads for the door,

"Do not worry F, I am coming for the Colonel."

Agency Headquarters Piedmont's Division

In Piedmont's over-sized office he and one of his subordinates are having a heart-to-heart conversation.

"Well, colonel you really fucked up this time."

"Shut up F."

"You just don't understand the can of whoop-ass you just unleashed on your own behind."

"F, you have no idea what's going on here boy, so I suggest you shut up, and hope she comes."

"Oh, she's coming, I have no doubt of that. What you gonna do when she comes for you."

"What's she going to do F? Look at all these monitors there's no place she can hide, I can see her anywhere in this complex. Noting she can do I won't see."

"You're sure about that Colonel? Want to bet your life on that sir."

Suddenly one by one the monitors start the blank out. Piedmont yells, "What the hell?! The monitors, they're all going blank!" he pauses for a moment, then points at F, "You! You son of a,,, what the hell did you do?"

F answers, Well since you asked so nicely I'll tell you a story Colonel."

A few days ago before F went to see Cj

In the private lab of Axel Grease Monkey F enters, "Hey Greasy did you get the jamming device done?"

He answers, "Yeah, well I got to thinking what you wanted me to do with it. You know these things are top of the line and have a hundred percent success rate,,, than I thought, they don't work against our own tech. So I'm guessing you wanted me to modify one for you. So here you go F."

"Thanks Greasy, you're a life saver."

"True F, true."

As F is leaving the room, Grease Monkey adds, "Oh, one more thing F… Kick his ass."

F answers "We will Greasy, we will."

After hearing F's story he speaks, "You fools gave her a Modified jamming device that works on our tech, I should've known you would do something like this!!"

F replies, "How dare you sir, to imply that I would conduct in such flow play. You, sir, have insulted my honor. I never said I handed to her. Haha."

"Shut up F! Shut the hell up!!"

BANG! BANG! BANG! Slice! Swing!
Slice! Boom! Plop! Drop!

"F what was that? What was that?"

He answers,
"Oh, you mean the sounds of machine
gun fire, slicing, dicing, and bodies
hitting the floor? That's most likely the
men that killed Kirk last night."

BANG! BANG! Slice! Swing! Drop!
"That's must be the three goons that
jumped me in my hotel room."

BANG! Slice! Drop! "And that's the last
of your personal guards biting the dust.
Well, that means you're next Colonel,

and it couldn't happen to a nicer asshole."

Piedmont collected his composure and calmly sat down at his desk awaiting for Axel to enter, his wait was short as she wasted no time.

She walks in staring Piedmont down while she uses her dagger to cut F from his bonds. relieved he says,

"Thanks Cj, glad you could make it in time, the colonel was losing it."

She responds, "When I am done, he will have nothing left to lose. And my name is Axel."

Piedmont speaks, "Well finally, you see things my way Agent Axel."

She answers, "All I want to see is your blood all over my blade you bastard. You killed my husband."

Piedmont chuckles as he explains, "Your husband-to-be worked for me, oh yes." as he continues talking, she closes her eyes trying to get a vision of what happened last night.

Kirk's house last night, Cj has already left the room while Kirk grabs a rifle from a secret panel as he turns he sees Piedmont,

"You? What are you doing here? This was not the plan."

Piedmont replies, "No it wasn't Agent Kirk. You were supposed to watch her and bring her back, not fuck her and keep her for yourself."

"I'm sorry Colonel, but I love h..." Kirk is cut off by the bullet entering his forehead.

Her eyes opens
As Piedmont stops talking, F asks, "You killed Kirk, got your night squad, and guards killed so you could have control over her." he answers,

"F Agent Axel's a weapon of mass destruction, and should be under our control. But no there's more to this she need to know because it's bigger than controlling her."

Axel puts her hand on her sword's handle saying, "Speak demon, say your last words so I can send you on the express to hell."

Piedmont reveals, "You don't get it Axel, this whole campaign wasn't about controlling you, it's about destroying you, taking you down. Yes, everything was done for this very moment. Ordering you to kill Agent Capricorn, your best friend, and sister agent."

Axel says, "No I've seen the evidence against her."

"What you saw has lies, that I created. I knew your sense of duty would blind you to the truth. You killed your friend over a lie." Agent Campbell and his daughter, I knew you were going to fail in protecting them. It was set for you to fail."

F jumps in, "We lost a lot of agents that day, how could you set us up like that."

"Yes F, most of those agents I had issues with, and I wanted them gone. Let's just say I was cleaning house, and more would have fallen if you didn't punk out."

F replies, "You son of a bitch."

"Oh, stop it F, this was a long time coming, two birds with one swing of a sharp blade. One breaking Axel and two killing some of the people I hated the most. Campbell, Kirk, and Major Blake Hall your father."

He throws photos at Axel she falls to her knees as she sees her parents dead with their heads sliced from their bodies. She cries out, "You monster!!!"

F says, "I can't believe you orchestrated all of this, you of all people."

Piedmont responds, "You're right F, I didn't,,, well not on my own." Just then his partner enters the room and walks to his side.

Axel's anger and rage turn to disbelief as she says, "Aj?"

Aj responds, "That's Empress bitch."

"But you are dead I killed you."
"In your dreams Cj, you cannot kill me. You are not strong enough."

Axel drops her head as the Empress continues, "I told you long ago that every man that loves you would die by my hand." She looks over at F saying, "Hello F, that means you are next, no man loved her more than you, even if she could not see it."

F says, "I still couldn't wrap my head around the fact that you wanted to do all this against the Agency."

Piedmont responds, "It was a fair-trade son. I help her get Axel and she'll give us all the data we need to keep all our country's enemies at bay. Hell boy, all the intel we're getting from Miss. Empress is an international espionage goldmine."

Empress punches her dagger into Piedmont from behind saying, "A goldmine you will never explore, for you made me out to be a liar, Kirk was to die by my hand, so I kill you so Cj can't have her revenge for his death Colonel."

She goes on "Now I'll kill the one man that loves you more than any other man has..." Axel looks towards "F" as Empress continues "...And you were too blinded by your misguided guilt to see the love you could have had..."

As she talks "F" eases back to grab a weapon, Empress throws her dagger as she continues, "...A love that you will never know!" the dagger stabs through F's tight, he yells, and falls back against the wall as her second dagger heads for his head...

But at the last second Daisy intercepted it. Axel steps between Empress and "F" saying, "I will not allow you to kill what is left of my heart, demon."

Empress responds, "Demon? I am the demon? Hahaha. Do you think that I am the villain of this story?"

She pauses for a moment, "Hahaha. You really do not remember what you have done to me do you?"

Puzzled F asks, "What the hell are you talking about? Cj what's she talking about?"

Axel tries to answer, "I, I, do not..."

Empress cuts her off, "Oh F, you do not understand the superpowers of a woman. We can shape, and mold reality around us and make it what we want it to be. We can make the truth into a lie, and the lie into the truth. We can change what is real and make it our truth and ignore what's real. No matter how much the world shows us we are wrong, in our minds we are right."

She focuses in on a shocked Cj saying, "Open the door Cj, go through it, and remember what really happened that day."

She removes the glove from her left hand to show Cj as she continues, "Remember what you did to me."

Cj's closes her eyes as her mind takes her back to the hallway where Dj and the others angrily point toward the door, she goes over opens it, and walks in.

A burst of bright light flashes as she hears Aj's voice, **"Through the door Cj and stop living your truth and see The Truth."**

The cave in Korea many years ago.
Bj has just run out not wanting to be sold as an assassin now Aj is sent to bring Bj back.

A few minutes later Cj is sent after them.

Bj is standing near the cliff looking over the horizon. From behind he hears Aj,

"The master sent me to bring you back." he turns to her saying, "Well what are you going to do."

She smiles and runs into his arms, and they kiss, she says,

"Your plan worked, but we need to leave here quick."

He replies, "Yes let us go and start a new life together."

They kiss again, but is cut short when they hear Cj,

"You traitors, you betrayed the Clan, you both are unfit to be in the Clan."

Bj yells, "Cj wait!" too late as she throws her dagger at his head, but Aj uses the palm of her hand to catch it, she cries out in pain which causes her to slip off the edge of the cliff, Bj grabs her and pulls her up to the edge.

Cj challenges, "Bj stand up and face me so I can run you through like the coward you are."

He tells Aj, "Hold on tight to the edge, I love you so much."

Aj responds, "No no no Bj, she will kill you."

He stands up to face Cj, "You do not have to do this Cj. We can all run away together. All of us. We can all be happy together"

She reacts, "All of us? You mean Dj is a part of this too? All you traitors must die."

Bj says, "Please Cj try to under..." Before he could finish, she rams her sword through his cheat.

Aj yells, "Bj!!!" as she continues hanging on the cliff's edge. Cj picks up her dagger, she hears Dj voice from behind,

"Cj? "Master sent me to bring you all back, but what happened here?" He yells once he sees Cj throwing her dagger at him,

"Cj! Nooo!" Cj pushes Bj's body off the cliff as Aj screams, "Bj!!!" Aj tries to pull herself up, but Cj stomps her foot in Aj' face causing her to lose her grip and she too falls. Cj goes over to Dj to finish him off, and again he screams,

"Cj!! Noooo!!!"

Axel's eyes open but she's in a daze as Empress tells the rest of the story.

"Yes, Cj you killed Bj and Dj. You thought you killed me, but I survived the fall, but hitting the waters was rough. It took me hours to recover myself and find Bj's body so I could bury him. After I laid Bj to rest I started bleeding. You caused me to miscarry.

First, you took the man I loved, then you took our child. I wanted to see you dead I vowed to avenge the deaths of my family. I vowed to end you, Cj."

Axel falls to her knees crying, "I'm sorry! I'm sorry!! Please forgive me!!!

She drops her head as she continues to gravel as Empress raises her sword high about to behead Axel saying,

"Apology accepted Cj."

She's about to strike F yells, "Nooo!!!" he rips the dagger from his leg and throws it, the blade slices into Empress's neck cutting her windpipes, she falls backward to the floor dying in a pool of her own blood.

He yells, Cj! Cj! Axel snap out of it!"

He slowly limps toward her. Axel goes over to Empress still crying and begging for forgiveness.

Empress reaches for Axel's hand, Axel receives her blood-soaked hand saying, "I am sorry, I am so, so sorry."

F stands over them saying,

"Cj she's dying in her own blood… Axel, she's suffering you have to end it,,, now."

Empress/Aj closes her eyes as Axel/Cj ends her suffering.

F places his hand on Cj's shoulder saying, "It was the right thing to do"

She lays her head against Aj's body and continues to cry.

Sometime later at The Place

Cj and F have laid Aj to rest. She stands over the resting site staring not saying much. F breaks the silence,

"Are you sure we did the right thing by not dissolving her body with the chemicals like we do with our fallen agents?"

She answers, "Enough of that, for now on this will be a true resting site for us and our enemies as well. No more liquidations."

He responds, "That's all good, but do you think the powers that be will go for that?"

She answers, "I will convince them."

He asks, "Uh Cj all the things you told me about your past, was any of it true? Did she really do all those bad things to you when you were kids?"

She answers, "Yes, but there is more to it… The why she would attack me. It was Bj. Every time she would attack me, it was because I was flirting with him in some kind of way. She always loved him,,, But I loved him too. That day I thought he was going to run away with me. When I saw the two of them kissing,,, I snapped and killed them and Dj."

F asks, "And Dj, what about him?"

She responds, "I never loved little Dj like that, he was just a little brother to me. When I said I loved him like a future husband. I was just creating a truth that I could live with in my head."

F says, "Oh, well I hate to break your mood of confusion, but I really need my leg tended to."

"By the way F, here is your blue-light gizmo, thanks it really helped."

"You're welcome now I can use it to get my thigh stitched up."

"I will do it F."

"You stitching me up? Now that's a twist, I can't wait to see that."

"It will be fine F."

She stops and pauses, smiles asking, "What is the F for anyway?"

He answers, "Oh, my name it's Ferdinand, Ferdinand Fox."

She smiles saying, "Ah, Ferdinand… I like it."

She kisses him.

In pain, he says, "Ouch, uh can we go now?"

They leave with her helping him as his limp has gotten a bit worse.

They continued their conversation laughing as they fade into the misty moonlight.

End

Epilogue

Back at Agency's Headquarters

Cj is patching up F's leg,

"Nice stitch work on the thigh Cj. I'm very impressed."

She replies, "I had some practice, and besides did you really think I was going to mess your leg up?"

He answers, "To tell the truth, I didn't know what to think babe. Remember I was always the one doing the patch jobs around here."

Just then a voice responds to his words

"Well that's good to know soldier."

They both look towards where the voice came from. By the door, Grease Monkey with the one who spoke. Six foot five, two hundred and twenty pounds of solid man with white hair and attitude.

"Agent Axel, Agent Fox. My name is Kane, Cornelius Kane. I'm the new commander around here. I heard a lot about you two, I hope you're ready to start dishing out some real Hash Justice."

F speaks, "Hum, imagine that."

Cast:

Axel aka Cj…………………………………Jay Clan, US Agent
Empress aka Aj……………...Jay Clan, World Class Assassin
"F" aka Ferdinand………………………US Agency Support
Kirk Landing…………………………………...Cj's Husband
The Master…………………………...Leader of the Jay Clan
Bj…………………………………….…..Jay Clan Assassin
Dj…………………………………….…..Jay Clan Assassin
Colonel Piedmont…………...US Agency Division Commander
Bart Campbell………………………………...US Agent
Bella Campbell……………………………….US Agent
Major Blake Hall………………………………Cj's Father
Mrs. Blake Hall………………………………Cj Mother
Axel Grease Monkey……………………Agency's Mechanic
Capricorn……………………………………...US Agent
Ej………………………………………….…..Jay Clan Assassin

Mid-Credits

Deep underground in one of the Agency's hidden labs.

A strange operation has just concluded. The guinea pig,,, uh patient has just woke up. She hears a voice from a loudspeaker calling her name,

"Agent Campbell. Agent Bella Campbell." she answers,

"Yes, yes I'm awake."

The door opens as a woman walks in.

"Hello Agent Campbell, I' Doctor Carla Albright."

Bella asks jokingly, "Give it to me straight doc, am I going to make it?"

Albright answers, "Very much so agent, but for now, I need you to get out of that bed and stand up."

Bella responds, "I can't, I lost the use of my arms and legs."

Albright responds, "That being the case when you first got here, but now you can stand. Now get up!"

As she works her way up to her feet, Albright explains, "You now have new

arms and legs. You can stand, walk, run,
and punch stuff.”

Bella makes it to her feet, she’s
checking out her new limbs as Albright
continues talking,

“Now you can run faster, jump higher,
and hit harder. Congratulation Campbell.
You’re our first Bionic Agent.”

Bella smiles.

CODE NAME: AXEL

Welcome to New Breed Publishing, Home of Paperbacks, Comics, Mags, Audio, and E-Books packed full of Action, Adventure, Fantasy, and Horror. Great Stories, Heroes, and Monsters are all here for your Entertainment and Escapism. Welcome to the fun, the excitement, the mysteries, the all-out chaos, and the greatest adventures. Welcome to the New Breed.

Be Sure To Check out Some of Our Other Books.

<u>Out Now</u>

Shadow When Evil Walks

Night on the Haunted Highway

Project Daybreak

Find them at Amazon, Barnes & Noble, Apple iTunes, Google Play and other outlets

CODE NAME: AXEL

You Can Find New Breed Books at

1920 Sparkman Drive Suite 5
Huntsville, AL 35816
256-270-7296

CREAMERCACHE@GMAIL.COM

eBay   CREAMERCACHECOMICS

whatnot   CREAMER_CACHE

facebook   CREAMERCACHECOMICS

instagram   CREAMER_CACHE_COMICS

<u>Up Next</u>
Powerstar Earth's Mightiest Hero
Powerstar Coloring Book
Powerstar Black and White
World of the New Breed

<u>Coming Soon</u>
Shadow Chronicles of Evil
Night on the Haunted Highway Beatty's
Brigade

Thunder Bird
The Reap

New Breed Ratings Chart

To insure our readers safe enjoyment, and peace of mind for parents as well we here at New Breed Publishing will be rating our books from here forward for your convenience and protection. Below is our standard Ratings Chart

G: General for all ages
PG: Parental guidance
PG-13: May be inappropriate for under 13
M: Mature Readers
R: Restricted parents are advised
RR: Very Restricted Strongly advised
RRR: May be to Harsh for even Mature readers

Post Credits
Korea, the cave

The Clan Master and some other members have just brought back the body of the Empress/Aj from America.

Some of them begin to chant as a figure fades from the shadow.

The master speaks, "Mongo Smalls, You have returned, as you said."

He replies, **"Yes Clan leader."**

"Then you are here for us to revive Aj the Empress back to life again?"

"No, she has been reanimated twice already, both deaths by the hands of Cj, who killed her again for a third time. This poor soul had done as I needed and she had suffered enough on this plane. I used her to challenge one of my many champions, so let Aj finally rest and find her peace now. She's earned it."

"As you wish Smalls, as you wish."

As Smalls fades back into the shadows he concludes,

"You have done well Jay Master, you've helped me to prepare for the coming Conflict, now be as you once were as I take my leave."

MARK W. LESLIE

CODE NAME: AXEL

copyrights

209

9 798224 837182